D1444312

ONCE UPON A QUARANTINE

M.C. BEHM

ILLUSTRATED BY SWAPAN DEBNATH

Treehouse Publishing | Saint Louis, MO 63116

Treehouse Publishing | Saint Louis, MO 63116

For information, contact:
Treehouse Publishing
An imprint of Amphorae Publishing Group
a woman- and veteran-owned business
4168 Hartford Street, Saint Louis, MO 63116

Publisher's Note: This is a work of fiction. Any real people or
places are used in a purely fictional manner.

Manufactured in the United States of America
Set in Adobe Caslon Pro
Interior and cover layout by Kristina Blank Makansi
Illustrations: Swapan Debnath

Library of Congress Control Number: 2020943890
ISBN: 9780996390187

To those who have battled the virus monster and everyone who sacrificed to protect and provide for others.

Once upon a quarantine,
we all were stuck at home.

A virus monster prowled
the streets in search
of human bones.

"What does it want? Why does it hurt?"
Our kids just **had to know.**

The monster stalked our cities
and shuttered restaurants.

It conquered all our public spaces with

taunts

and

taunts

and

taunts.

"I'VE COME,"

it roared.

"YOU BETTER HIDE.
YOU BETTER TURN AND RUN.
I'LL CLOSE YOUR TOWN!"

It STOMPED and STORMED.

"NO SCHOOL. NO FRIENDS.
NO FUN!"

"I'LL SPLIT YOU UP,"

the virus said.

"BY RELIGION, RACE AND CLASS.
I'LL MAKE YOU DOUBT EACH OTHER,
LIKE YOUR HATREDS OF THE PAST."

So, we all did as we were told,
shut doors and tied loose ends.

We didn't hug, high five, or greet
our neighbors or our friends.

Each night we gathered round the news
and felt increasingly alone.
We called family.
We tried to work.

We learned to
Zoom by phone.

14

Then something changed,
something

big

that brought the whole world hope.

Heroes flew with masks and scrubs,
with gloves and stethoscopes.

16

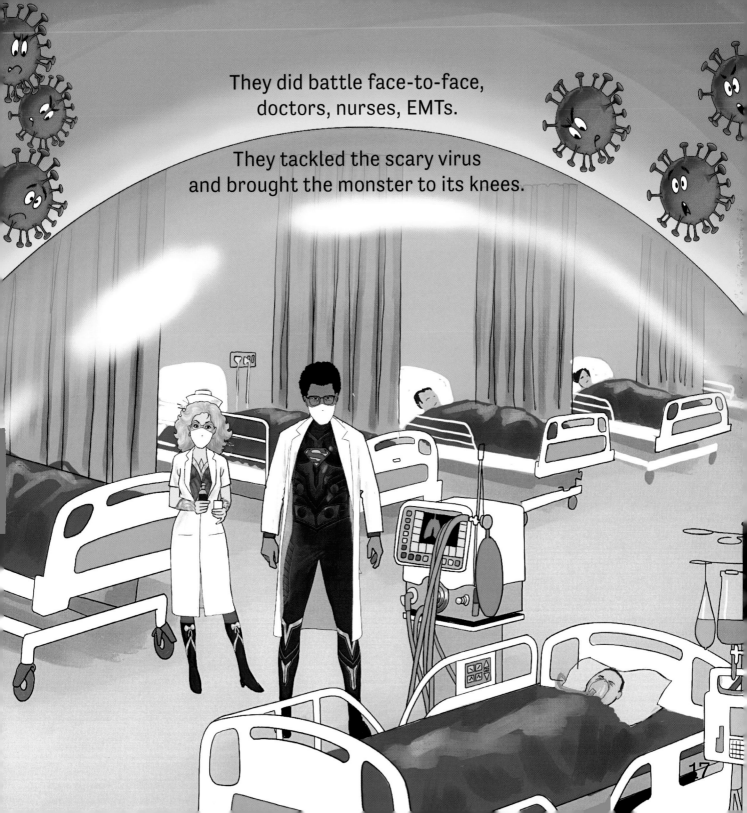

They did battle face-to-face,
doctors, nurses, EMTs.

They tackled the scary virus
and brought the monster to its knees.

17

Still others bravely ventured out,
giving food and stocking shelves.
They made sure we
got our groceries,
never thinking
of themselves.

18

An army of essential workers
kept the whole world functioning,
not afraid of any monsters,
just like Martin Luther King.

While at home, we finally had the time
to cook
and bake
and read.

We did puzzles.
We played board games,
and planted garden seeds.

"But when will the big, bad virus end?"
our kids looked up and said.

S is for Science

"When will the superhero scientists make sure that monster's dead?"

Camouflaged in white lab coats,
they rushed onto the scene,
using data-driven analysis
to develop a vaccine.

24

We stepped outside and looked around.
The earth was clean and green.
The air was clear and skies were bright,
thanks to our quarantine.

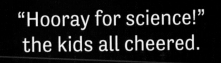

"Hooray for science!"
the kids all cheered.

"Hooray for medicine!
And hooray for all who battled
so we could play again."

Back to life, we opened our eyes
and saw the world had changed.
The virus made us realize
how we are all the same.

WHAT IS COVID-19?

Covid-19 is a virus that makes you sick and was first seen in people in the year 2019. It is very transmissible, meaning that it can easily spread from person to person with a cough or a touch. Doctors and scientists have worked hard to learn everything there is to know about Covid-19, such as how to treat people who are sick with the virus and how to stop the virus from spreading.

HOW IS A VACCINE MADE AND WHAT DOES IT DO?

The huge goal of lots and lots of scientists around the world is to make a drug that will keep people safe from Covid-19. Just like the measles or chickenpox, these viruses can be stopped with a vaccine which teaches the body how to beat the disease. Usually a vaccine is produced by taking a small amount of the actual virus and making it safe, so it won't be able to grow inside a human body. Then that small and safe amount is given to people so that their bodies can practice fighting the disease and build immunity.

WHY DID WE HAVE TO QUARANTINE?

Schools and non-essential businesses were closed, and families were asked to stay at home all around the world. While this wasn't a full quarantine with zero outside contact, by staying home and not working we all reduced our number of contacts and made it so the virus could not spread as quickly. Throughout history there have been many quarantines to keep healthy and sick people separate from each other. By slowing down the spread of Covid-19, doctors, nurses, and everyone in the medical field could work with fewer sick patients at a time and save more lives.

Author's Note

Once Upon A Quarantine was written early on during our home isolation amidst a backdrop of schoolwork-hostage negotiations, toilet-paper-maximization tutorials, and deep-pantry-diving dinners. The story grew out of a desire to do something positive and helpful in the face of suffering. Profits from sales of *Once Upon A Quarantine* will go to the Boys and Girls Club. During the COVID-19 crisis our Local Club donated over 7,000 free meals to children in need in our community. Money raised by this book will go towards continuing the Club's great work.

Acknowledgements

This book would not be possible without the help of many people. Carol Swartout Klein, who wrote *Painting for Peace in Ferguson*, my wife and principal editor Jayme Miller, and Treehouse Publishing. Also, my daughter Mackenzie, who added spunk and creativity to the story.

About the Author

M.C. Behm is a former public school history teacher in urban west Philadelphia where he received a Master's in Education from the University of Pennsylvania. He writes the Tahoe Dad column for the *Reno Gazette Journal* and the *Tahoe Mountain News*. In addition to *Once Upon a Quarantine*, Behm wrote *The Elixir of Yosemite*, a murder mystery which explores the origins of modern environmentalism through rock climbing adventures. He lives in California with his family.
www.behmbooks.com

About the Illustrator

Swapan Debnath is a self-taught artist based in Kolkata, India who has illustrated over 200 children's books. His cartoons have been printed in India's leading newspapers and magazines such as Anandabazar Patrika, Woman's Era, and Alive. During his boyhood, Swapan wished for more colorful depictions in books. He felt the lack of pictures was like a home without a window. Since then, he has endeavored to spread delight though his artwork.
swapandebnath1007@gmail.com